FORTUNATELY, THE MILK

NEIL GAIMAN

ILLUSTRATED BY
CHRIS RIDDELL

BLOOMSBURY

LONDON OXFORD NEW YORK NEW DELHI SYDNEY

Bloomsbury Publishing, London, Oxford, New York, New Delhi and Sydney

First published in Great Britain in September 2013 by Bloomsbury Publishing Plc
50 Bedford Square, London WC1B 3DP

First published in the United States by HarperCollins Children's Books
a division of HarperCollins Publishers, 195 Broadway, New York, NY 10007

www.bloomsbury.com

This paperback edition published in June 2014

A CIP catalogue record for this book is available from the British Library

ISBN 978 1 4088 4179 2

Printed and bound in China by Leo Paper Products, Heshan, Guangdong

9 10 8

BOOKS BY NEIL GAIMAN FROM BLOOMSBURY

NOVELS

The Sleeper and the Spindle
Fortunately, the Milk
The Graveyard Book
Odd and the Frost Giants
Coraline

SHORT STORIES

M is for Magic

PICTURE BOOKS

Illustrated by Dave McKean
Crazy Hair
The Day I Swapped My Dad for Two Goldfish
The Wolves in the Walls

Illustrated by Charles Vess
Instructions
Blueberry Girl

Illustrated by Gris Grimly
The Dangerous Alphabet

Illustrated by Adam Rex
Chu's Day
Chu's First Day at School
Chu's Day at the Beach

GRAPHIC NOVELS

Illustrated by Dave McKean
Signal to Noise
The Tragical Comedy or Comical Tragedy of Mr Punch
MirrorMask

Illustrated by P. Craig Russell
Coraline
The Graveyard Book: Volume One
The Graveyard Book: Volume Two

For my late father, David, who would have told the tale
with delight, and for my son, Michael, who would never
have believed a word of it. With love.
N.G.

For Jack
C.R.

There was only orange juice in the fridge. Nothing else that you could put on cereal, unless you think that ketchup or mayonnaise or pickle juice would be nice on your Toastios, which I do not, and neither does my little sister, although she has eaten some pretty weird things in her day, like mushrooms in chocolate.*

* She did not actually like eating them. And I had not actually told her that there were mushrooms inside the chocolate. It was an experiment.

'No milk,' said my sister.

'Nope,' I said, looking behind the jam in the fridge, just in case. 'None at all.'

Our mum had gone off to a
conference. She was presenting a
paper on lizards. Before she went, she
reminded us of the important things
that had to happen while she was away.

My dad was reading the paper. I do not think he pays a lot of attention to the world while he is reading his paper.

'Did you hear me?' asked my mum, who is suspicious. 'What did I say?'

'Do not forget to take the kids to
Orchestra Practice tomorrow; it's
Violin on Wednesday night; you've
frozen a dinner for each night you're
away and labelled them; the spare

house key is with the Nicolsons; the plumber will be here on Monday morning and do not use or flush the upstairs toilet until he's been; feed the goldfish; you love us and you'll be back on Thursday,' said my father.

I think my mum was surprised. 'Yes, that's right,' she said. She kissed us all. Then she said, 'Oh, and we're almost out of milk. You'll need to pick some up.' After she went away, my dad had a

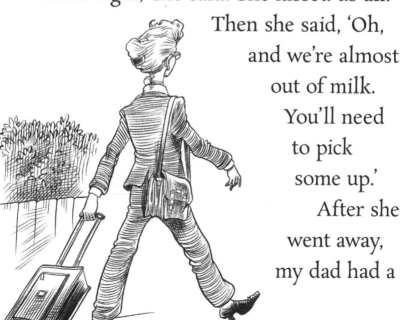

cup of tea. There was still some milk left.

We defrosted Meal Number One, but we made a bit of a mess of things, so we went to the Indian restaurant. Before we went to sleep, Dad made us mugs of hot chocolate to make up for the whole Missing of Mum.

That was last night.

Now Dad came into the kitchen. 'Eat your cereal,' he said. 'Remember, it's Orchestra Practice this afternoon.'

'We can't eat our cereal,' said my sister, sadly.

'I don't see why not,' said my father.

'We've got plenty of cereal. There's Toastios and there's muesli. We have bowls. We have spoons. Spoons are excellent. Sort of like forks, only not as stabby.'

'No milk,' I said.

'No milk,' said my sister.

I watched my dad think about this. He looked like he was going to suggest that we have something for breakfast you do not need milk for, like sausages, but then he looked like he remembered that, without milk, he couldn't have his tea. He had his 'no tea' face on.

'You poor children,' he said. 'I will walk down to the shop on the corner. I will get milk.'

'Thank you,' said my sister.

'Not skimmed,' I told him. 'That stuff tastes like water.'

'Right,' said my dad. 'Not skimmed.' He went out.

I poured some Toastios into a bowl. I stared at them. I waited.

'How long has he been?' asked my sister.

'Ages,' I said.

'I thought so,' said my little sister.

We drank orange juice. My sister practised her violin. I suggested that she stop playing her violin, and she did.

My sister made faces at me.

'How long has it been now?' she asked.

'Ages and ages,' I told her.

'What happens if he never comes back?' she asked.

'I suppose we eat the pickles,' I said.

'You can't eat pickles for breakfast,' said my sister. 'And I don't like pickles at any time. What if something awful has happened to him? Mum would blame us.'

'I expect he just ran into one of his friends at the corner shop,' I said, 'and they got talking and he lost track of time.'

I ate a dry Toastio as an experiment. It was sort of OK, but not as good as in milk.

There was a *thump* and a *bang* at the front door, and my father came in.

'Where have you been all this time?' asked my sister.

'Ah,' said my father. 'Um. Yes. Well, funny you should ask me that.'

'You ran into someone you knew,' I said, 'and you lost track of time.'

'I BOUGHT THE MILK,' said my father. 'And I did indeed say a brief hello to Mister Ronson from over the road, who was buying a paper. I walked out of the corner shop, and heard something odd that seemed to be coming from above me. It was a noise like this: *thumm-thumm*.

I looked up and saw a huge silver disc hovering in the air above Marshall Road.

Hullo, I said to myself. *That's not something you see every day.* And then something odd happened.'

'*That* wasn't odd?' I asked.

'Well, something odder,' said my dad.

'

THE ODD THING was the beam of light that came out of the disc – a glittery, shimmery beam of light that was visible even in the daylight. And the next thing I knew, I was being sucked up into the disc. Fortunately, I had put the milk into my coat pocket.

The deck of the disc was metal. It was as big as a playing field, or bigger.

"We have come to your planet from a world very far away," said the people in the disc.

I call them "people", but they were
a bit green and rather globby and they
looked very grumpy indeed.

"Now, as a representative of your

species, we demand that you give us ownership of the whole planet. We are going to remodel it."

"I jolly well won't," I said.

"Then," one of them said, "we will bring all your enemies here and get them to make you miserable until you agree to sign the planet over to us."

I was going to point out to them that I didn't have any enemies when I noticed a large metal door with

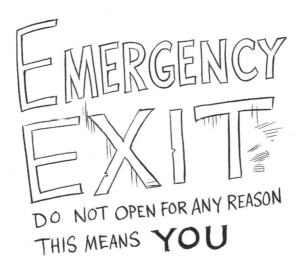

EMERGENCY EXIT
DO NOT OPEN FOR ANY REASON
THIS MEANS **YOU**

on it. I opened the door.

"Don't do that," said a green globby person. "You'll let the space-time continuum in."

But it was too late – I had already pushed open the door.

I jumped.

I was falling.

Fortunately, I had kept tight hold of the milk, so when I splashed into the sea I didn't lose it.

"What was that?" said a woman's voice. "A big fish? A mermaid? Or was it a spy?"

I wanted to say that I wasn't any of those things, but my mouth was full of seawater. I felt myself being hauled up on to the deck of a little ship. There were a number of men and a woman on the deck, and they all looked very cross.

"Who be ye, landlubber?" asked the woman, who had a big hat on her head and a parrot on her shoulder.

"He's a spy! A walrus in a coat! A new kind of mermaid with legs!" said the men.

"What are you doing here?" asked the woman.

"Well," I said. "I'd just been to the corner shop for some milk for my children's breakfast and for my tea, and the next thing I knew –"

"He's lying, Your Majesty!"

She pulled out her cutlass. "You dare lie to the Queen of the Pirates?"

Fortunately, I had kept tight hold of the milk, and now I pointed to it.

"If I did not go to the corner shop to fetch the milk," I asked them, "then *where* did this milk come from?"

At this, the pirates were completely speechless.

"Now," I said, "if you could let me off somewhere near to my destination, I would be much obliged to you."

"And where would that happen to be?" said the Queen of the Pirates.

"At the corner of Marshall Road and Fletcher Lane," I said. "My children are waiting there for their breakfast."

"You're on a pirate ship now, my fine bucko," said the Pirate Queen. "And you don't get dropped off anywhere. There are only two choices – you can join my pirate crew, or refuse to join and we will slit your cowardly throat and you will go to the bottom of the sea, where you will feed the fishes."

"What about walking the plank?" I asked.

"Never heard of it!" said the pirates.

"Walking the plank!" I said. "It's what proper pirates do! Look, I'll show you. Do you have a plank anywhere?"

It took some looking, but we found a plank, and I showed the pirates where to put it. We discussed nailing it down, but the Pirate Queen decided it was safer just to get the two fattest pirates to sit on the end of it.

"Why exactly do you want to walk the plank?" asked the Pirate Queen.

I edged out on to the plank. The blue Caribbean water splashed gently beneath me.

"Well," I said, "I've seen lots of stories with pirates in them, and it seems to me that if I'm going to be rescued –"

At this the pirates started to laugh so hard their stomachs wobbled, and the parrot took off into the air in amazement.

"Rescue?" they said. "There's no rescue out here. We're in the middle of the sea."

"Nevertheless," I told them, "if you are going to be rescued, it will always be while walking the plank."

"Which we don't do," said the Pirate Queen. "Here. Have a Spanish doubloon and come and join us in our piratical adventures. It's the eighteenth century," she added,

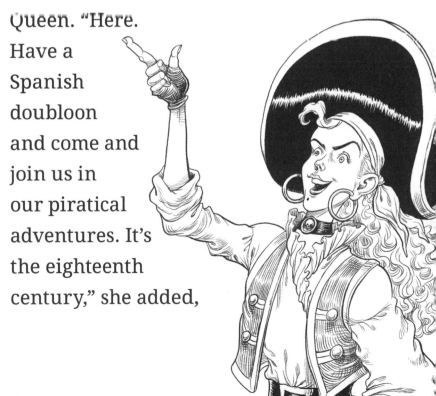

"and there's always room for a bright, enthusiastic pirate."

I caught the doubloon. "I almost wish that I could," I told her. "But I have children. And they need their breakfast."

"Then you must die! Walk the plank!"

I edged out to the end of the plank. Sharks were circling. So were piranhas –'

And this was where I interrupted my dad for the first time. 'Hang on,' I said. 'Piranhas are a freshwater fish. What were they doing in the sea?'

'You're right,' said my father. 'The piranhas were later. Right. So . . .

'I WAS OUT at the end of the plank, facing certain death, when a rope ladder hit my shoulder and a deep booming voice shouted, "Quickly! Climb up the rope ladder!"

I needed no more encouragement than this, and I grabbed the rope ladder with both hands. Fortunately, the milk was pushed deep into the pocket of my coat. The pirates hurled insults at me, and even discharged pistols, but neither insults nor pistol-shot found their target and I soon made it to the top of the rope ladder.

I'd never been in the basket of a hot-air balloon before. It was very peaceful up there.

The person in the balloon basket said, "I hope you don't mind me helping, but it looked like you were having problems down there."

I said, "You're a Stegosaurus!"

"I am an inventor," he said. "I have invented the thing we are travelling in, which I call Professor Steg's Floaty-Ball-Person-Carrier."

"I call it a balloon," I said.

"Professor Steg's Floaty-Ball-Person-Carrier is the original name," he said. "And right now we are one hundred and fifty million years in the future."

"Actually," I said, "we are about three hundred years in the past."

"Do you like hard-hairy-wet-white-crunchers?" he asked.

"Coconuts?" I guessed.

"I named them first," said Professor Steg. He picked up a coconut from a basket and ate it, shell and all, just as you or I might crunch toast.

He showed me his Time Machine. He was very proud of it. It was a large cardboard box with several pebbles on it, and stones stuck to the side.

There was also a
large, red button. I
looked at the stones.
"Hang on," I said.
"Those are diamonds.
And sapphires.
And rubies."

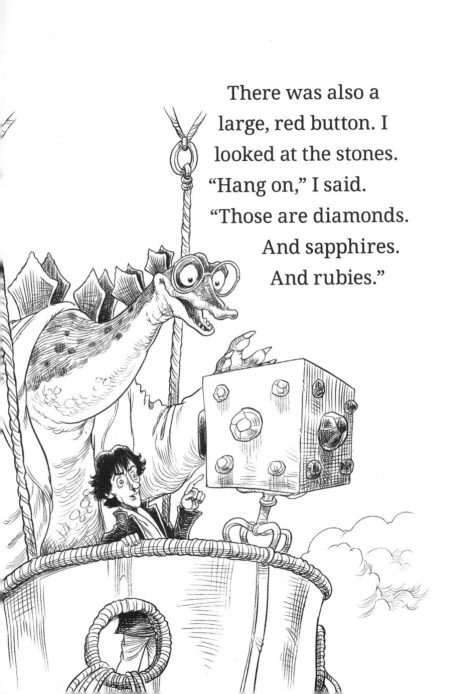

"Actually," he said, "I call them special-shiny-clear-stones, special-shiny-bluey-stones, and, um –"

"Special-shiny-red-stones?" I suggested.

"Indeed," he said. "I called them that when I was inventing my Really-Good-Moves-Around-in-Time-Machine, one hundred and fifty million years ago."

"Well," I told him, "it was very lucky for me that you turned up when you did and rescued me. I am slightly lost in space and time right now and need to get home in order to make sure my children have milk for their breakfast." I showed it to him. "This is the milk. Although I expect that one hundred and fifty million years ago you called it 'wet-white-drinky-stuff'."

"Dinosaurs are reptiles, sir," said Professor Steg. "We do not go in for milk."

"Do you go in for breakfast cereal?" I asked.

"Of course!" he said. "Dinosaurs LOVE breakfast cereal. Especially the kind with nuts in."

"What do you have on your cereal?" I asked.

"Orange juice, mostly. Or we just eat it dry. But I shall put this in my book. *In the distant future, small mammals put milk on their breakfast cereal.* I shall write a wonderful book, when I return to the present."

"Actually," I said, "I think this is definitely the past. It has pirates in it."

"It's the future," he said. "All the dinosaurs have gone off into the stars, leaving the world to mammals."

"I wondered where you all went," I said.

"The stars," he told me. "That is where we will have gone."

"So," I said. "Can you take me home?"

"Well," he said. "Yes and no."

"What does that mean?"

"Yes, I would love to take you home. Nothing would make me happier. No, I cannot take you home. In all honesty, I do not believe that I can take *me* home. My Time Machine is being temperamental. I need a special-shiny-greeny-stone. I have pressed that button many times but nothing happens."

"*Button?* Don't you mean 'big-red-flat-pressy-thing'?" I asked.

"I most certainly do not. It is a button. I named it after my Aunt Button."

"Can I press it?"

"If you wish."

I pressed the button. The sun shot around the sky, and the sky started to flicker in nights and in days, and the balloon began to rock and lurch and zoom around like an angry fly.

I held on to the ropes as hard as I could. Fortunately, I was still keeping tight hold of the milk in my right hand.

When we stopped being blown all across the sky, it was night and, according to Professor Steg, we had only gone back about a thousand years. The moon was nearly full.

"I am *even* further from my children and our breakfast," I said.

"You have your milk," he said. "Where there is milk, there is hope. Ah, over there. That looks like a perfect landing platform for time-travelling scientists in Floaty-Ball-Person-Carriers."

We landed on the platform and got out. The platform stuck up out of the jungle and had flaming torches on each side. There were people standing on it with very black hair and sharp stone knives.

"Is this a balloon-landing platform?" I asked the people.

"It is not," said a fat man. "It is our temple. We had a very bad harvest last year and we had just asked the gods to send us a sacrifice, to make sure that this year's harvest is better, when you floated down in that thing, with your monster."

"Thank you, by the way," said a little thin man. "I was going to be the sacrifice if no one else turned up. Much obliged."

"So now we will sacrifice you and your monster."

"But my children are waiting for their breakfast," I said. "Look!" I held up the milk.

"Why did they all just fall to their knees?" asked Professor Steg. "Is this usual hairless mammal behaviour? Perhaps I should hold up some hard-hairy-wet-white-crunchers and see what happens."

"Coconuts!" I told him. "They are called coconuts!"

"What is that you are holding?" the fat man asked.

"Milk," I said.

"Milk!" they exclaimed, and they prostrated themselves on the ground.

"We have a prophecy," said the fat man, "that when a man and a spiny-backed monster descend from the skies on a round floaty thing –"

"Floaty-Ball-Person-Carrier," said the little thin man.

"Yes. One of those. We were told that when that happened, if the man held up milk then we were not to sacrifice them but we were meant to take them to the volcano, and give them, as a present, the green jewel that is the EYE of SPLOD."

"Splod?"

"He is the god of people with short, funny names."

"It is," I said, "a remarkably specific sort of a prophecy. When did you receive it?"

"Last Wednesday," said the fat man, proudly. "The Priest of Splod was woken in the night by a voice whispering from the heavens. And when he went to look and see who it was, there was nobody there. Also, he was sleeping on the top of the temple, and nobody else could have been up there with him. So it must have either been Splod himself talking, or one of his angelic messengers."

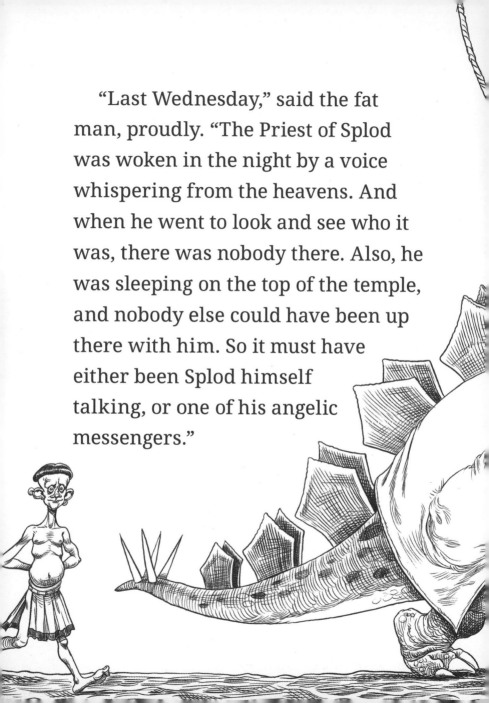

We walked together down a jungle
path. Professor Steg held the rope
in his mouth that led up to the
balloon, and he dragged
the balloon along.

After half an hour we reached the volcano.

It was not a very big volcano. There were wisps of smoke coming from the top of it.

On the side of the volcano there was a carving of a big, scary face with one eye in the middle of its forehead. The eye was the biggest emerald I had ever seen.

"A special-shiny-greeny-stone!" said Professor Steg, with his mouth full of rope.

The fat man clambered up the side of the volcano.

"It is a good thing that Splod himself told us to give you the EYE of SPLOD," said the little thin man who had narrowly avoided being sacrificed, "because there is another prophecy that says if the EYE of SPLOD is ever removed, Great Splod will awaken and spread burning destruction across the land."

"Here you go," said the fat man.

He handed us the emerald.

Professor Steg nipped up the rope

ladder into the balloon's basket and began to install the emerald in the Time Machine.'

'Hang on. He was a Stegosaurus?'
'Yes.'
'Then how could he just nip up a rope ladder?'
'He was,' said my father, 'a large Stegosaurus, but very light on his feet. There are fat people who are excellent dancers.'
'Are there any ponies in this?' asked my sister. 'I thought there would be ponies by now.'

'I WAS STANDING on the ground, holding on to the rope ladder, when the ground shook and the very small volcano began to belch smoke and lava.

"Splod is angry!" shouted the little thin man. "He wants his eye back."

There was a rushing wind, and the balloon jerked me up into the air, high above the splurting lava.

Unfortunately, I dropped the milk. I wasn't holding on to it tightly enough. It landed on the top of Splod's head.

Professor Steg hauled the rope ladder up with his tail.

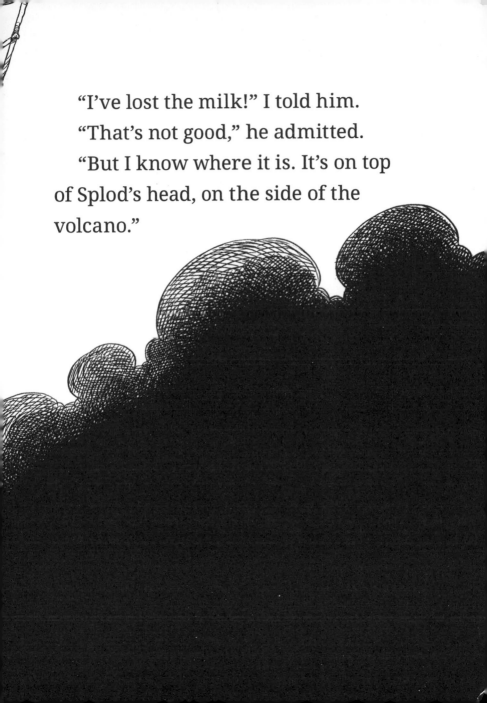

"I've lost the milk!" I told him.

"That's not good," he admitted.

"But I know where it is. It's on top of Splod's head, on the side of the volcano."

Professor Steg said, "Good Splod! What on earth is that?"

Before our eyes, another balloon, just like ours, appeared over by the volcano. A man hurried down the rope ladder. He placed a large emerald in Splod's eye, picked up the milk from Splod's head, ran up the ladder, and the balloon vanished.

The very small volcano stopped erupting as suddenly as if it had been turned off.

"That was a bit peculiar, wasn't it?" said the professor.

"It was," I agreed, gloom and despair and despondency overcoming me. "That man in that balloon stole my milk. We are lost in the past, with jungles and pirates and volcanoes.

Now I will never get home. My children will never have breakfast. We are doomed to float for ever through the dusty air of the past in a hot-air balloon."

"It is not a balloon," said Professor Steg. "It is a Floaty-Ball-Person-Carrier. What nonsense you do talk. Now, I think *that* should do the trick."

He finished attaching the emerald to the box, using string, mostly, and also sticky tape, and he pushed the red button.

"Where are we going?" I asked. It seemed like the sun was zooming across the sky, as if nights were following days in a flickering strobe.

"The far, far future!" said Professor Steg.

The machine stopped.

We were hanging in the air above a grassy plain, with a very small grey mountain beneath us.

"There," said Professor Steg. "It is now an extinct volcano. But look!"

On the side of the extinct volcano was carved the face of Splod, still recognisable, even though it was much eroded by time and the weather, and in the single eye was a huge green emerald, a perfect twin to the one that we had attached to the Time Machine.

"Right," said Professor Steg. "Grab me that special-shiny-greeny-stone."

I went over the side of the basket and down the rope ladder. I pulled the emerald out of the eye socket.

Below me, on the plain, a number
of brightly coloured ponies were
gathered, and when I picked up the
emerald one of them shouted up at
me. "You must be the man without the
milk. We have heard about you in our
tales."

"Why are you a pink pony with a pale blue star on the side?" I asked.

"I know," said the pony with a sigh. "It's what everybody's wearing these days. Pale blue stars are *so* last year."

Professor Steg leaned over the side of the balloon's basket. "Hurry up!" he called. "If the volcano is going to go off, it could do it any moment."

The volcano made a noise like a huge burp, and the middle of it collapsed into itself.

"We thought it would do that," said a green pony with a sparkly mane.

"There was a prophecy, I suppose," I said.

"No. We're just very clever." All the ponies nodded. They *were* very clever ponies.'

'I am so glad there were ponies,' said my sister.

I GOT BACK INTO the balloon basket. Professor Steg unhooked the first emerald from his Time Machine and replaced it with the one that I had just taken from the weathered face of Splod-in-the-Future.

"Do not, whatever else you might do," said the professor, "touch those two stones together."

"Why not?"

"Because, according to my calculations, if the same object from two different times touches itself, one of two things will happen. Either the Universe will cease to exist. Or three remarkable dwarfs will dance through the streets with flowerpots on their heads."

"That sounds astonishingly specific," I said.

"I know. But it is *science*. And it is much more probable that the Universe will end."

"I thought it would be," I said.

"You look so sad," Professor Steg told me.

"I am! It's the milk. My children are breakfastless –"

"The milk!" said Professor Steg. "Of course!" And with that, Professor Steg pressed the red button with his heavily armoured tail.

There was a *zoom*, a *tworp*, and a *thang*, and we were hurtling through the cosmic void.

And then it was dark.

Very dark.

"Oops,"

said Professor Steg.

"Overshot a little. Only by a week, though. Hold on . . ."

Professor Steg leaned over the side of the basket.

"Excuse me?" he said. "Is there anyone around?"

"Only me," said a very surprised-sounding voice from below us. "The Priest of Splod. Who is that up in the sky? Is it a bird? You do not sound like a bird."

"I am not a bird," said Professor Steg. "I am a marvellous yet mysterious and prophetic voice, telling you a mighty prophecy. So mighty that . . . Um . . . Very mighty indeed. Listen. When a huge and good-looking spiny-backed individual –"

"Monster," I told him. "The

prophecy said monster."

"Accompanied by a scrawny human being of revolting appearance –" said Professor Steg.

"That was not necessary."

"– lands in a Floaty-Ball-Person-Carrier, you must not sacrifice them. You must instead take them to the volcano and give them the EYE of SPLOD. And this shall be the way that you shall know them. The human being will hold up some milk."

"Is that the prophecy?" said the voice.

"Yes."

"Is there anything about crops in it?"

"I'm afraid not."

"Oh well. Thanks anyway, prophetic and mysterious voices from the air."

I pressed the red button.

Daylight.

We were in the middle of a very familiar volcanic eruption.

"Quickly!" I said. "Give me the emerald!"

A little way away, I could see a balloon being blown through the sky, while fire and ash were swept around it by the wind. I could see me in the balloon, standing next to Professor Steg, with my mouth open. I looked miserable.

Professor Steg – *my* Professor Steg – gave me the emerald.

I raced down the rope ladder and placed the emerald back into the face's eye. Then, as the volcano stopped

erupting, I looked around
for the milk. I knew it had
landed on Splod's head
when it fell.

Fortunately, the milk
had fallen into a small drift
of volcanic ash, and was
unharmed.

I picked it up, brushed it
off, and started back up the
balloon's ladder. Professor
Steg pressed the button.

The sky went dark.

We were floating above a landscape of ominous towers and disquieting castles. It was not a friendly place. Bats flew across the sky in huge flocks, crowding out the waning moon.

"I don't like this place," I told the professor.

"I don't see why not," he said. "It looks as if it would be very nice when the sun comes up."

There was a loud *FLUT!* and, where the bats had been fluttering, several pallid people were now standing. The man in front had a very bald head. They all had sharp teeth.

"Ve are wumpires," they said. "Vot is this? Who are you? Answer us, or ve vill wiwisect you."

"I am Professor Steg," boomed the Stegosaurus. "This is my assistant. We are on an important mission. I am trying to get back to the present. My assistant is trying to get home to the future for breakfast."

At the word "breakfast" all the wumpires looked very excited.

"Ve have not had our breakfast," they told us. "Ve normally have viggly vorms, vith orange juice on them. Orange juice makes vorms ewen vigglier. Like vandering spaghetti. But if ve cannot eat vorms ve vill eat assistant, or even roast professor."

One of the wumpires took out a fork, and looked me up and down in a hungry sort of way.

The baldest, most bulging-eyed, rattiest of the wumpires said, "Vot is this box?"

"It is my finest invention," began Professor Steg, proudly, but I interrupted.

"It is to keep sandwiches in," I said.

"Sandviches?" said the wumpire.

"Sandwiches," I said, with as much certainty as I could muster.

"Ve thought it vos a Time Machine," said the head wumpire, with a sly, sharp smile. "And ve could use it to inwade the vorld!"

"Definitely sandwiches," I told him.

"Vot happens if I press this button, then?" asked a lady wumpire. She had long black hair that

covered most of
her face, and
peered out
at the world
with one
suspicious eye.
She pressed the
button. We went
forward six
hours in time.
"See?" said the
professor, happily.
"All this place needs to brighten it up
is a little bit of sunshine."

The head wumpire said, "Vot?" and
dissolved into a cloud of oily black
smoke. So did all his friends.

"Yes," I said. "It is a nice place here, after all. In the daylight."

The professor tinkered with the jewels and the string and the buttons. Then he said, "I think I've got it properly fine-tuned, now. This next press should bring you back to your own time, place, and breakfast."

But before the tip of his tail could touch the button, a voice said, "I'll explain later. Fate of the world at stake."

A hand grabbed, and the milk,
which I had carried safely for so long,
was gone. I turned in time to catch a
glimpse of a fine-looking gentleman
with his back to me, holding my milk,
and then the hole in space through
which he had reached was
closed.

"My milk!"

"He said he'd
explain later,"
said the professor.
"I'd be inclined to
believe him."

The hole in space
opened again. A voice
shouted, "Catch!"

and the milk came rocketing through.

Fortunately, the milk struck me in the stomach, and in clutching my hands to my belly I caught the milk.

"There," said the professor. "Everything is back to normal."

"He did say he'd explain later," I pointed out. "And that wasn't much of an explanation."

"But it's not later yet," said Professor Steg. "It's still now. It won't be later until later."

He was arranging pebbles and stones and string on the top of the Time Machine box. "Final coordinates entered," he said. "And then it's off to your house for breakfast."'

'Does that mean that there is a Stegosaurus in a hot-air balloon outside?' I asked my dad.

'There is not,' he said. 'For reasons that will become apparent.'

'I think that there should have been some *nice* wumpires,' said my sister, wistfully. 'Nice, handsome, misunderstood wumpires.'

'There were not,' said my father.

"WOULD YOU LIKE to press the button?" said Professor Steg.

I pressed the red button. There was an ear-popping noise and a flicker of years and I was floating, in a balloon basket, above the corner of Marshall Road and Fletcher Lane. I could see our house from above. I could see the bicycles in the back garden. I could see the rabbit hutch.

"We're here!" I said, and I patted Professor Steg on the back ridge-plates.

"It was very nice, having you as a

travelling companiAARGH,"
said the professor, because there
was a familiar sort of a *thumm-
thumm* noise, and, before I had
a chance to press the red button, we
were deposited, balloon
and all, on the
enormous metal
deck of a flying
saucer, with a
number of very
grumpy-looking
green globby
people staring at
us with too many
eyes. They did not
look pleased.

"Ha-*HA!*" said several green globby people at the same time. "You thought you had escaped from us! And you were wrong! Now, you must sign the planet over to us so that we can remodel it. We will take out all the trees, for a start, and put in plastic flamingos."

"Why?"

"We like plastic flamingos. We think they are the highest and finest art form that Earth has achieved. And they are tidier than trees."

"Also, we are going to replace the clouds with scented candles."

"We like scented candles too," explained a huge green globby person, who looked like he was mostly made of snot.

"We also like decorative plates!" said another. "We will put a decorative plate up where the moon is now."

"A really *big* decorative plate, showing landmarks of the world." "And we will then replace all the landmarks of the world with decorative plates with pictures of landmarks on them too, so the Eiffel Tower will be replaced by a large plate with a picture of the Eiffel Tower on it.

And Australia will be replaced by a really seriously big plate with Australia on it."

"Also, we will replace all of your mountains with embroidered cushions," said the smallest, globbiest thing of all, with triumph in its glutinous voice.

"We have learned a lot from our previous meeting," said some globs that were sticking to a wall. "If you look over there, you will see that the door to the space-time continuum you used to escape through last time is now securely locked."

It was definitely locked. It had a huge padlock on it, and a sign saying

on it, in unfriendly red letters. There were also chains around it, a tape that said

DO NOT CROSS

and a handwritten notice that said

for your Convenience, Please Use Another Door.

Escape
was impossible.

"Also, we have
depowered your
Time Machine."

I looked at
the professor. His
armoured back-flaps
were drooping, and
his tail was – well, not
actually between his legs, because
Stegosauruses aren't made that way,
but if they were, it would have been.

"We have been tracking your
movements through time and space,"
said a large globby alien in front of a
console with a screen on it.

"Now, see what happens when I press this grundledorfer," said a particularly drippy alien. It was half sticking to the wall, next to a large, black shiny button.

"It's called a button," I said.

"Nonsense. We named it after our brood-aunt, Nessie Grundledorfer," said the globby aliens. The particularly drippy alien pressed the black button on the metal wall with something that might have been a finger and might just have been a long strand of snot.

There was a *crackle*.

There was a *fizz*.

Standing around us, in attitudes
of anger and irritation, were several
pirates, some of the black-haired people
from the jungle, a very unhappy-
looking volcano god, a large bowl filled
with piranhas, and some wumpires.'

'I'm not sure that I understand what the piranhas are doing,' said my sister.

'They were from a narrow escape earlier that I forgot to mention,' said our father. 'Fortunately, the milk floated at a crucial moment and it all ended for the best.'

'I thought it might,' I said.

"U H-OH," I said.

"Prepare to be keelhauled, you scurvy dogs," shouted the pirates.

"Let us now sacrifice them both to great Splod!" shouted the people with shiny black hair.

"They stole my eye! Twice!" rumbled mighty Splod.

"Ve vants those willains and warmints wiolently vound up," proclaimed a tall lady wumpire with long fingernails.

The piranhas said nothing, but they thrashed about in their bowl, ominously.

"Doomed," moaned Professor Steg. "We cannot escape. They have frozen us in time and depowered us. Even my mighty Time Machine can do no more than open a small window in time and space – smaller than either of us could get through."

"But can you do it?" I asked. "Open a little window in time to our last location?"

"Of course. But what good would that do?"

"Quickly!" I said. "Do it!"

Professor Steg pushed the button on the box with the tip of his nose.

There was a *zum!* and a *plip!* and a window opened in space and time, large enough for an arm to get through.

I reached into it.

"I'll explain later," I said. "Fate of the world at stake." I grabbed the milk from me, fifteen minutes earlier, through the tiny space-time portal.

"You must like milk a lot," said the globby aliens. "But that craving for lactic liquids will not make us take pity on you or let you go, and spare your badly designed planet."

"It should," I said. "What am I holding in my left hand?"

"Er. The milk," they said.

"And what am I holding in my right hand?"

They paused. Then one alien, so green and small and so globby and crusted that he might have been an enormous snot-bubble blown by an elephant with a terrible head-cold, said, ". . . The same milk from fifteen minutes earlier."

"Exactly," I said. "Now. Think about this one very carefully. What would happen if I touched these two things together?"

The globby aliens went a very pale green. The pirates, shiny-black-haired people and the piranhas looked at them, puzzled, seeking some kind of explanation, as did the wumpires.

"If two things that are the same thing touch," proclaimed the volcano god, "then the whole Universe shall end. Thus sayeth the great and unutterable Splod."

"How does a volcano know so much about trans-temporal meta-science?" asked one of the pale green aliens.

"Being a geological formation gives you a lot of time to think," said Splod. "Also, I subscribe to a number of learned journals."

I coughed, in what I hoped was an ominous sort of way. "Well?" I asked.

"What he said," admitted the green globby aliens. "The bit about the Universe ending."

"So," I told them. "Unless you wish to spend the rest of your lives in a

Universe that no longer exists, you had better return things to the way they were. And then go away."

The aliens looked at each other. They grinned at each other.

One of them pressed the grundledorfer.

The wumpires, pirates, piranhas, volcano god, and the worshippers of the volcano god were gone.

"What if," suggested one of the green globby aliens, hopefully, "we only redecorated the southern hemisphere?"

"Not a chance," I said. "Now, release us, or the milk touches itself! And then go away. Leave this planet for ever."

The aliens looked at me, then they

looked at each other, and then they sighed, with a noise like a hundred elephantine snot balloons all deflating at once.

"Right," they said.

It was at that moment that a voice louder than anything I have ever heard – and I had heard a volcano erupt at very close range – said,

"GALACTIC POLICE. DO NOT MOVE."

My hands shook, but the milk did not touch the milk, and the Universe did not end.

There were red and blue flashing lights and then, stepping off their space-bikes, there were about half a dozen uniformed dinosaurs, holding unmistakably large and extremely serious weapons. They pointed their weapons at the green globby aliens.

"You are charged with breaking into people's planets and redecorating them," said a noble and imposing-looking Tyrannosaurus rex. "And then with running away and doing it again somewhere else, over and over. You have committed crimes against the inhabitants of eighteen planets, and crimes against good taste."

"What we did to Rigel Four was

art!" argued a globby alien.

"Art? There are people on Rigel Four," said an Ankylosaurus, "who have to look up, every night, at a moon with three huge plaster ducks flying across it."

Something very long with a head on the end of it came over to us. It was attached to a very large body, on the other side of the room. "Who are you?" it asked Professor Steg. "And why is your gorilla holding a trans-temporally dislocated milk container?"

"I am not a gorilla," I said. "I am a human father."

"The human is holding the milk in order to make these evil redecorating snot-bubbles go away and stop menacing this planet and us," said Professor Steg.

The Diplodocus in a police cap opened its mouth and didn't say anything.

The Tyrannosaurus, who had handcuffed all of the green globby people together with something that looked a lot more like pink string-in-a-can than it looked like handcuffs, which was a good thing because they probably didn't have hands and they definitely didn't have wrists, looked at us and his eyes opened wide.

"Great day in the morning!" he exclaimed. "A biped. A Stegosaurus. A Floaty-Ball-Person-Carrier . . ." And he stopped, as if unable to go on.

A Pteranodon flapped over to

us, then landed at Professor Steg's feet. It looked up at him, and said, hesitantly, "Would you be . . . ? Could you be . . . ? The inventor of Professor Steg's Pointy-Zooming-into-Outer-Space-Machine – of Professor Steg's Really-Good-Moves-Around-in-Time-Machine? Would you be the author of *My Travels into the Extremely Far Future and What I Found There*? Professor Steg, wisest of all dinosaur-kind? Madam, is it truly you?"

"It is," said the professor. (*Madam?* I thought, embarrassed.) "And this is my assistant."

The Pteranodon extended a wing tip for me to shake, and, without thinking, I moved the second milk from my right hand to my left . . .

Where the first milk was.

Everybody gasped.

Unfortunately, the milk that had been in my right hand, which was the same as the milk that was already in my left hand, the same milk fifteen minutes apart *touched each other.*

I held my breath.

There was a fizzing noise, and a mewing as if a hundred kittens were being agitated in an enormous basket.

Professor Steg closed her eyes.

"I can't look," she said.

Three purple dwarfs with flowerpots on their heads appeared from nowhere and began to do a little dance.

"Did the Universe end?" said the Tyrannosaurus, with his eyes tightly scrunched closed.

"Look!" I said.

We all watched the dwarfs dance. They weren't human and they weren't dinosaurs. They had purple skin and orange beards, and the flowerpots on their heads had lots of flowers growing out of them. They did a complicated sort of a dance, with lots of leg kicking and shouts of "*Oi!*" and "*Olay!*" and "*Pertung!*" And then, as strangely as they had come, they vanished.

"Ah," said Professor Steg. "It was always a possibility that this might happen. And fortunately, the Universe has not ended."

She pressed the button again, with her tail. A small hole in space and time opened up. I was standing on the other side with a baffled expression on my face.

"Catch!" I shouted, and threw the milk through the hole. As the portal closed, I saw me catch the milk using my stomach.

The green globby aliens having been rounded up and taken away, all the space dinosaurs gathered around.

"I can't believe it," said the Diplodocus. "Professor Steg. Just like in the comics. The dinosaur who taught us that, in the far future, small mammals will eat their breakfast cereal with milk on it. Inventor of the button. She's here, in front of us, with her gorilla."

"Not a gorilla, but

a human father," said Professor Steg, and all the other dinosaurs gasped and said things like "How wise she is!" and "What a brain!" and "How can you tell the difference between that creature and a gorilla? Is it the shoes?"

Professor Steg said, "This human father has been my companion on my strange journey into the future. Now, before I take my leave of him, and come with you, O Space Dinosaurs, we should sing to him one of the great old dinosaur songs."

They sang me a song in six-part harmony called "How Do You Feel This Morning When You Know What You Did Last Night?" Then they sang me a song called "Don't Go Down to the Tar Pits, Dear, Because I'm Getting Stuck on You". The Galactic Police dinosaurs sang me a song about being Galactic Police and saving people all over the Universe, and driving very fast space-bikes. And then they all sang a song called "I've Got a Loverly Bunch of Hard-Hairy-Wet-White-Crunchers", which was an ancient dinosaur song that had apparently been written by Professor Steg's Aunt Button.

There is nothing in the whole of creation as beautiful as dinosaurs singing in harmony.

"Now," said Professor Steg, "I shall go off in my Floaty-Ball-Person-Carrier, with my newfound Dinosaur Space Patrol friends, and I shall explore the Universe, and then I shall return to my own time, and write a book about it."

"You actually write several books," said the Diplodocus. *"Professor Steg's Guide to Everything in the Whole of the Future* was my favourite. It's very inspirational."

I said goodbye to all the dinosaurs. I thanked Professor Steg for saving my life.

"Not at all," she said. "We were both fortunate that you had the milk with you. It is not every container of milk that saves the world, after all."

"That was me that saved the world," I said. "Not the milk."

The space dinosaurs all had their pictures taken holding the milk and smiling at the camera.

"What are you going to do with the milk?" they asked me. "Are you going to put it in a museum?"

"No, I am not," I told them. "I am going to give it to my children for their breakfast cereal. And possibly I will pour some in my tea."

Professor Steg nipped back up the rope and climbed into the basket of her balloon. The last I saw of her – of any of them – the whole inside of the flying saucer was fading into light so bright I had to close my eyes and look away.

And then I was standing at the back door of our house, none the worse for wear. Fortunately, the dinosaurs had

given me back the milk after they had
their photos taken with it.

So I came in.

And here I am.'

That was what
my dad said.

I looked at my sister and my sister
looked at me.
Then we both
looked around the
kitchen. At the
calendar on the
wall with the
hot-air balloons on it. At my dinosaur
models and my sister's ponies, at my
sister's vampire books, at
the picture of a volcano
I had painted when I
was little, last year, and
which is still up on the
wall by the fridge.

We looked at those things, and we looked at my dad.

'You know, we don't believe any of this,' said my sister.

'We don't,' I told him. 'Not any of it.'

'Especially not how you saved the world from being remodelled. Or the pirates.'

'Not. Any. Of. It,' I said.

My father shrugged. 'Suit yourselves,' he said. 'But it was all true.

And I can prove it.'

'How?'

'Yes. How?' asked my little sister.

'Well,' said my father, putting it down on the kitchen table, 'here's the milk.'

And he went back to reading his paper.

CHRIS RIDDELL, the artist, is a very mysterious and secretive person. When we asked him how he imagines the peculiar things that Mr Gaiman asks him to draw, he told us that he had no imagination whatsoever, but that he was fortunate in having excellent models, and in drawing all his characters from life. He then sent us the following drawings of his models for the story you have just read.

Having looked at these drawings, we found ourselves with several unanswered questions. How did Mr Riddell know the names of the various characters he had drawn? And for that matter, how would it be possible to draw ancient pirates, future ponies and galactic space police dinosaurs without access to a time machine of his own? We wrote to Mr Riddell, asking him these questions, but our letter was returned with the words 'GON AWAY' written on it in something that appeared to be fish paste.

The Publishers

SPLOD
THE
GOD

OF PEOPLE
WITH SHORT,
FUNNY NAMES